The Big, Big Wall

The Big, Big Wall

Reginald Howard
Illustrated by Jose Aruego and
Ariane Dewey

Green Light Readers
Harcourt, Inc.
Orlando   Austin   New York   San Diego   Toronto   London

Humpty Dumpty sat on a wall.

He did not want to have a big fall.

One friend came to the big, big wall.

"I will help you. You will not fall."

"Oh, not you. You look too small."

Two friends came to the big, big wall.

"We will help you. You will not fall."

"Oh, not you. You look too small."

Three friends came to the big, big wall.

"We will all help you. You will not fall."

Humpty Dumpty smiled at his friends.

"Now I can come back down again."

Walk With Me

Humpty Dumpty's friends worked together to help him get down from the wall. Work together with a friend in this game.

1 Stand beside your friend.

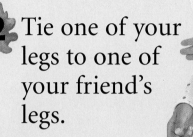

2 Tie one of your legs to one of your friend's legs.

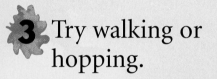

3 Try walking or hopping.

What happens?

What did you learn about working together?

Meet the Illustrators

Ariane Dewey has lots of rabbits visit her yard. She loves to watch them nibble dandelions. Ariane thought about those rabbits as she painted the rabbit in *The Big, Big Wall*. She says that cheery colors make her feel good. She hopes her purple rabbit and colorful animals make you happy, too.

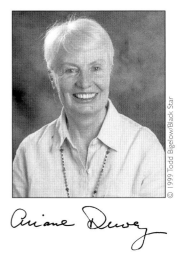

Jose Aruego had a pet pig named Snort when he was young. "I loved that pig!" Jose says. "He was so soft and funny." When Jose had to find a way to keep Humpty Dumpty from having a big fall, he thought about Snort. He decided that a pig would be a great cushion for Humpty Dumpty!

Requests for permission to make copies of any part of the work should be mailed
to the following address: Permissions Department, Harcourt, Inc.,
6277 Sea Harbor Drive, Orlando, Florida 32887-6777.

www.HarcourtBooks.com

First Green Light Readers edition 2001
Green Light Readers is a trademark of Harcourt, Inc., registered in the
United States of America and/or other jurisdictions.

The Library of Congress has cataloged an earlier edition as follows:
Howard, Reginald.
The big, big wall/by Reginald Howard; illustrated by Jose Aruego and
Ariane Dewey.
p. cm.
"Green Light Readers."
Summary: Humpty Dumpty's friends help him avoid a big, big fall.
[1. Eggs—Fiction. 2. Friendship—Fiction. 3. Stories in rhyme.]
I. Aruego, Jose, ill. II. Dewey, Ariane, ill. III. Title. IV. Green Light reader.
PZ8.3.H825Bi 2001
[E]—dc21 00-9724
ISBN 0-15-204813-8
ISBN 0-15-204853-7 (pb)

A C E G H F D B
A C E G H F D B (pb)

Ages 4-6
Grades: K-1
Guided Reading Level: C-D
Reading Recovery Level: 6-7

Green Light Readers
For the reader who's ready to GO!

"A must-have for any family with a beginning reader."—*Boston Sunday Herald*

"You can't go wrong with adding several copies of these terrific books to your beginning-to-read collection."—*School Library Journal*

"A winner for the beginner."—*Booklist*

Five Tips to Help Your Child Become a Great Reader

1. Get involved. Reading aloud to and with your child is just as important as encouraging your child to read independently.

2. Be curious. Ask questions about what your child is reading.

3. Make reading fun. Allow your child to pick books on subjects that interest her or him.

4. Words are everywhere—not just in books. Practice reading signs, packages, and cereal boxes with your child.

5. Set a good example. Make sure your child sees YOU reading.

Why Green Light Readers Is the Best Series for Your New Reader

● Created exclusively for beginning readers by some of the biggest and brightest names in children's books

● Reinforces the reading skills your child is learning in school

● Encourages children to read—and finish—books by themselves

● Offers extra enrichment through fun, age-appropriate activities unique to each story

● Incorporates characteristics of the Reading Recovery program used by educators

● Developed with Harcourt School Publishers and credentialed educational consultants

Daniel's Pet
Alma Flor Ada/G. Brian Karas

Sometimes
Keith Baker

A New Home
Tim Bowers

Rip's Secret Spot
Kristi T. Butler/Joe Cepeda

Cloudy Day Sunny Day
Donald Crews

Rabbit and Turtle Go to School
Lucy Floyd/Christopher Denise

The Tapping Tale
Judy Giglio/Joe Cepeda

The Big, Big Wall
Reginald Howard/Ariane Dewey/
Jose Aruego

What I See
Holly Keller

Down on the Farm
Rita Lascaro

Just Clowning Around: Two Stories
Steven MacDonald/David McPhail

Big Brown Bear
David McPhail

Big Pig and Little Pig
David McPhail

Jack and Rick
David McPhail

Come Here, Tiger!
Alex Moran/Lisa Campbell Ernst

Popcorn
Alex Moran/Betsy Everitt

Sam and Jack: Three Stories
Alex Moran/Tim Bowers

Six Silly Foxes
Alex Moran/Keith Baker

Lost!
Patti Trimble/Daniel Moreton

What Day Is It?
Patti Trimble/Daniel Moreton

Look for more Green Light Readers wherever books are sold!

How will Humpty Dumpty not have a big, big fall? Maybe his friends can help!

LEVEL 1
Buckle Up!
Getting Ready to Read

LEVEL 2
Start the Engine!
Reading with Help

Developed with Harcourt School Publishers, the leader in reading education

Green Light Readers
Harcourt, Inc.
525 B Street, San Diego, CA 92101
15 East 26th Street, New York, NY 10010
www.HarcourtBooks.com

Manufactured in China

$3.95 / Higher in Canada

ISBN 0-15-204853-7

04853

0 47132 00395 0

ISBN 0-15-204853-7

50395>

9 780152 048532

A Phonics-based Story

My Camp-Out

By Marcia Leonard
Photographs by Dorothy Handelman

LEVEL 1

REAL KIDS READERS

TM